The Fox in the Dark

By Alison Green

Illustrated by Deborah Allwright

ALISON GREEN BOOKS

Rabbit runs home.
　　He darts left and right,
Scampering, scrambling,
　　back through the night.
His ears flap, his tail bobs
　　– it's going to be tight! –
As he's chased by a fox
　　through the dark!

BANG! goes his door and

CLICK! snaps the latch.

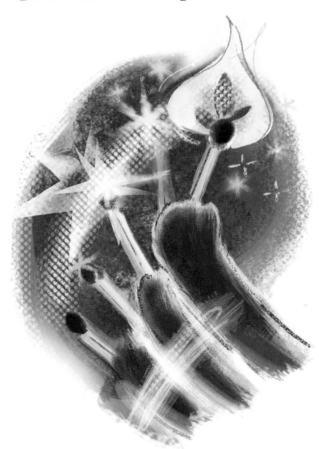

THUNK! goes the key and

SCRITCH! strikes a match,

And, "Phew!" Rabbit sighs,
"I've escaped! Not a scratch!
And I'm safe from that
fox in the dark."

But . . .

Rat-a-tat-tat!

Now, who can that be?

"Friend or fox?" Rabbit cries.
A voice quacks, "Look and see!
You'll never find anyone
more scared than me
Of the teeth of a fox in the dark!"

Rabbit peers round the door.
There's no fox – just a duck,
Who says, "Please let me in.
I've had so much bad luck.

My truck hit a ditch
and got stuck in the muck
And I've just seen
a fox in the dark."

Rabbit grumbles a bit.
   It's not really his habit
To share with a duck
   a bed made for a rabbit.

"The duvet's quite small," he says.
   "Try not to grab it,
While we hide from
   the fox in the dark."

Then . . .

Rat-a-tat-tat!

Who's that at the door?

"It's me!" squeaks a voice,
    "Is there room for one more?
I don't need much space,
    And my paws are so sore.
I've just run from a fox in the dark."

"Oh, really!" sighs Rabbit.
"The hour is so late!"
But the mouse stood outside
Is in such a sad state.
"I'm so tired," he says,
"I could hibernate,
Thanks to that fox in the dark!"

So they squoosh up together,
and Duck says, "Nice house!"

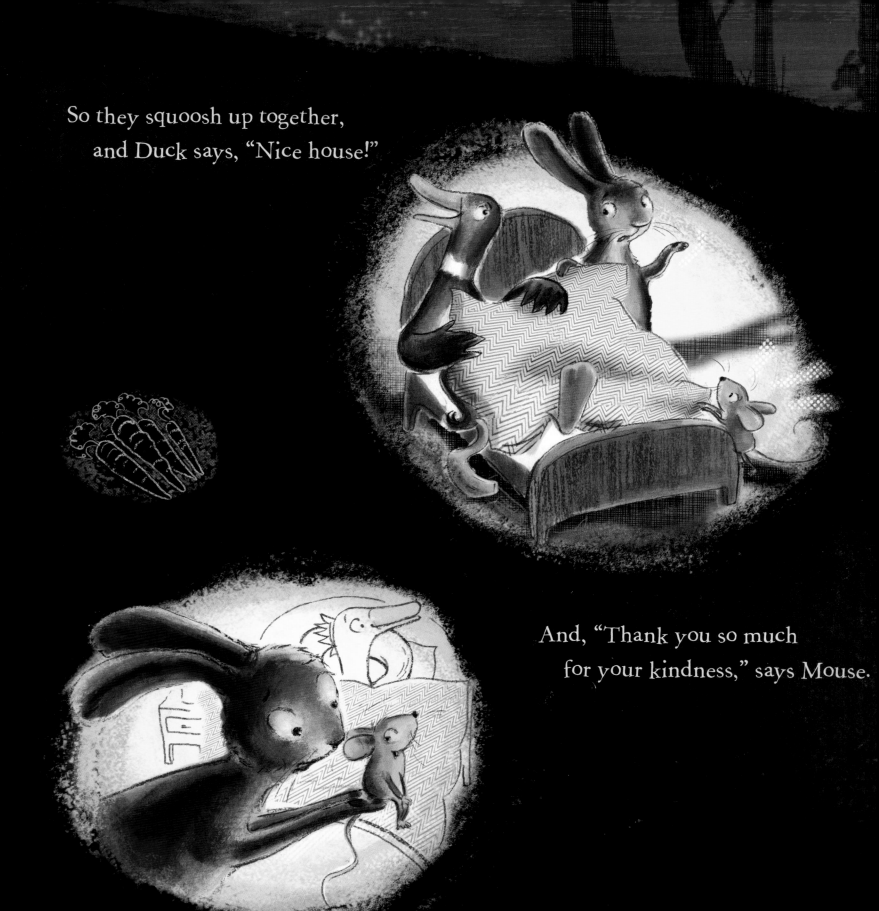

And, "Thank you so much
for your kindness," says Mouse.

And, "Sorry," says Rabbit,
"I ought not to grouse.
I'm just cross with that fox in the dark!"

But then . . .

Rat-a-tat-tat!

Who can that be now?
"If it's a horse, or a pig, or a cow,
They can just stay outside!"
Rabbit furrows his brow.
"I'll have words with
that fox in the dark!"

Outside is a lamb who
is shaking with fear.
"Please, may I come in?
It looks so safe in here.
A big, hairy, scary thing
barked in my ear,
And I'm sure it's
a fox in the dark!"

The bed is so full
    that it's starting to creak.
Rabbit shoves Mouse
    And Mouse gives a squeak.

Then Lamb accidentally
    squashes Duck's beak.
"Oh, drat that old fox in the dark!"

Then . . .

Rat-a-tat-tat!

comes a knock at the door.
"I'll get it!" says Duck
as he bumps to the floor.
"Not that there's room here
for **anyone** more!"

But outside is . . .

. . . A FOX IN

THE DARK!

"Don't eat us!" cries Duck.
"At least, please don't eat me!"
Rabbit and Lamb dive
behind the settee.
Mouse flings up a paw
and shouts, "I need a wee!"

. . . then Duck says,
    "He looks a bit **small** to me."
And the fox starts to cry and says,
    "Please help! You see,
I've lost my mum out in the dark."

"Just what I thought," says Duck.
"Ha! What a muddle!"

And Rabbit gives Foxcub
a very big cuddle.

Then Lamb takes a cloth and
cleans up Mouse's puddle:
"He gets scared by a fox in the dark."

Then . . .

Rat-a-tat-tat!

"Who's that now?" Rabbit sighs.
As he opens the door Duck says,
"That was unwise . . ."

For outside is a fox
    of a MUCH bigger size,
Looming down at them out of the dark!

But the Fox cries, "My baby!
I've searched for you so!"

"And you've found him," quacks Duck,
"So off you both go.
I don't like to rush you,
but as you well know,
A fox belongs out in the dark."

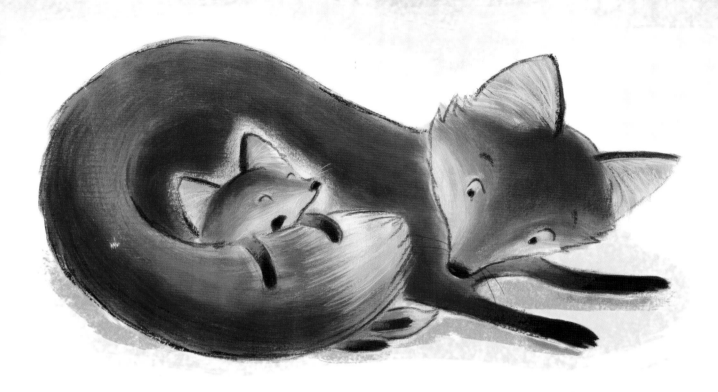

"We won't hurt you!" says Fox.
    "Oh, please let us stay!
You've all been so kind.
    We'll keep out of your way.
My baby's so tired.
    Our home's too far away
For a foxcub to trot in the dark."

But Rabbit cries out:
   "There's no room in the bed!
Where on earth will you sleep?"
   Mummy Fox shakes her head.
"Who needs a small bed?
   There's a big fox instead!
We can all snuggle up in the dark."

So they each grab what pillows
and rugs can be found.
Fox lies out comfortably
down on the ground.

Then they yawn and they stretch
And they all cuddle round
With the fox that came in from the dark.

For Nathalie, love Alison
For Logie and Florence, with love, D

First published in 2009 by Alison Green Books
An imprint of Scholastic Children's Books
Euston House, 24 Eversholt Street
London NW1 1DB
A division of Scholastic Ltd
www.scholastic.co.uk
London ~ New York ~ Toronto ~ Sydney ~ Auckland
Mexico City ~ New Delhi ~ Hong Kong

Text copyright © 2009 Alison Green
Illustrations copyright © 2009 Deborah Allwright

HB ISBN: 978 1 407103 93 8
PB ISBN: 978 1 407109 62 6
Printed in Singapore

1 3 5 7 9 10 8 6 4 2

Papers used by Scholastic Children's Books are made from wood grown in sustainable forests.